Sam's Seasons

Written by Christine Price
Illustrated by Winifred Barnum-Newman

STECK-VAUGHN
COMPANY
ELEMENTARY • SECONDARY • ADULT • LIBRARY

Sam, where are your boots?

Mom, do I have to find them today?
I don't remember where I left them.

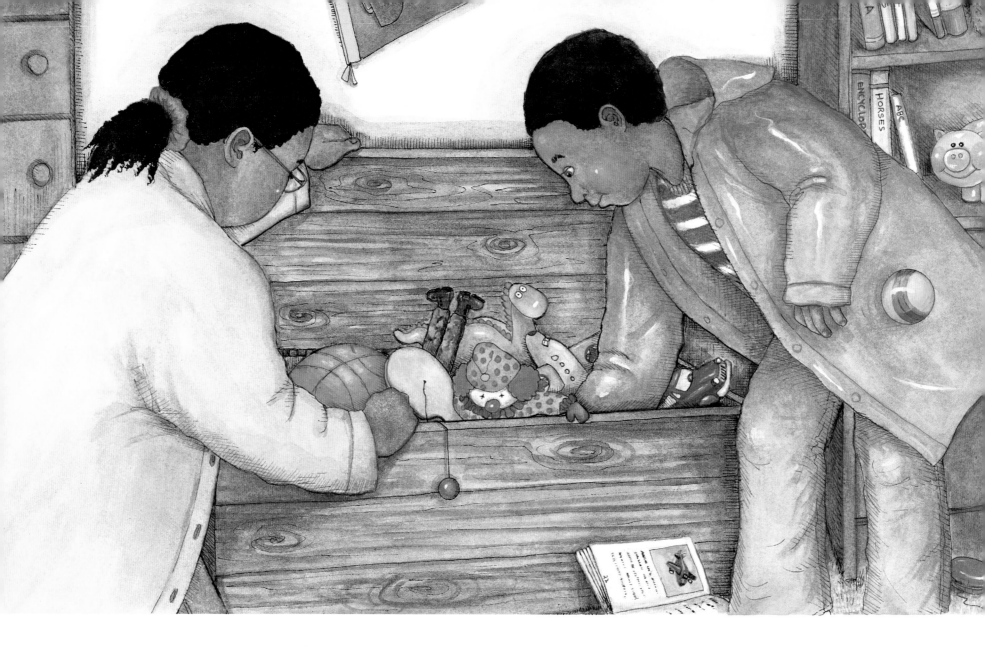

Sam, please find your boots.

 4

Last spring, I wore them in the rain.
I splashed in the water puddles.

Sam, please find your boots.

Last summer, I wore them to the beach.
I filled them with sand to make a castle.

Sam, please find your boots.

Last autumn, I wore them in the leaves.
I raked the leaves into a pile and jumped in.

 9

Sam, please find your boots.

Last winter, I wore them in the snow.
I used them to help stop my sled.

Sam, please find your boots.

They must be somewhere in here.
I know I wore them all four seasons.

But Sam, where are your boots NOW?

I found them!

But look, Mom, now my boots are too small.